Cat Club

Siamese

by Cameron L. Woodson

Bullfrog Books

Ideas for Parents and Teachers

Bullfrog Books let children practice reading informational text at the earliest reading levels. Repetition, familiar words, and photo labels support early readers.

Before Reading

- Discuss the cover photo. What does it tell them?
- Look at the picture glossary together. Read and discuss the words.

Read the Book

- "Walk" through the book and look at the photos. Let the child ask questions. Point out the photo labels.
- Read the book to the child, or have him or her read independently.

After Reading

- Prompt the child to think more. Ask: Siamese cats are very active! Can you think of other cat breeds that are active?

Bullfrog Books are published by Jump!
5357 Penn Avenue South
Minneapolis, MN 55419
www.jumplibrary.com

Library of Congress Cataloging-in-Publication Data

Names: Woodson, Cameron L., 1994– author.
Title: Siamese / Cameron L. Woodson.
Description: Minneapolis: Jump!, Inc., [2021]
Series: Cat club | Includes index.
Audience: Ages 5–8 | Audience: Grades K–1
Identifiers: LCCN 2019049902 (print)
LCCN 2019049903 (ebook)
ISBN 9781645274551 (hardcover)
ISBN 9781645274568 (ebook)
Subjects: LCSH: Siamese cat—Juvenile literature.
Classification: LCC SF449.S5 W66 2021 (print)
LCC SF449.S5 (ebook)
DDC 636.8/25—dc23
LC record available at https://lccn.loc.gov/2019049902
LC ebook record available at
https://lccn.loc.gov/2019049903

Editors: Jenna Gleisner and Susanne Bushman
Designer: Jenna Casura

Photo Credits: UroshPetrovic/iStock, cover; keyci13/iStock, 1; Kazantseva Olga/Shutterstock, 3; MelashaCat/Shutterstock, 4; Cressida studio/Shutterstock, 5; Altsva/Shutterstock, 6–7 (foreground), 23bl; ben bryant/Shutterstock, 6–7 (background), 23bl; Arco/P. Wegner/Age Fotostock, 8–9 (foreground); Evgeniya Uvarova/Shutterstock, 8–9 (background); Gerard Lacz/Age Fotostock, 10–11, 23bm; Juniors Bildarchiv GmbH/Alamy, 12, 23tm; Mediterranean/iStock, 13 (girl), 23tl; Jagodka/Shutterstock, 13 (cat), 23tl; Sari Oneal/Shutterstock, 14–15; Azel Bueckert/Shutterstock, 16, 23tr; vlalukinv/Shutterstock, 17; Titus Lacoste/Getty, 18–19, 23br; Zave Smith/Getty, 20–21; EEI_Tony/iStock, 22; Benjamaphon Duangpanta/Shutterstock, 24.

Printed in the United States of America at Corporate Graphics in North Mankato, Minnesota.

Table of Contents

Active Cats

This is a Siamese!

These cats have blue eyes.

Their heads are small.
But they have big ears!

Fur on their bodies is light.

Their faces, legs, tails, and ears are darker.

This is called a point pattern.

Cool!

Their bodies are long. They are thin, too. So are their tails!

Siamese are very active.

They pounce!

These cats are curious.

They love toys.

We play!

These cats can be noisy.

Meow!

They like to be up high.

This one sits on a perch.

Some climb trees!

I pet her.
She purrs!

Would you like a Siamese?

A Siamese Up Close

A Siamese has short fur and a long, thin body and tail. Its head is small, and its ears are large. Take a look at its other body parts!

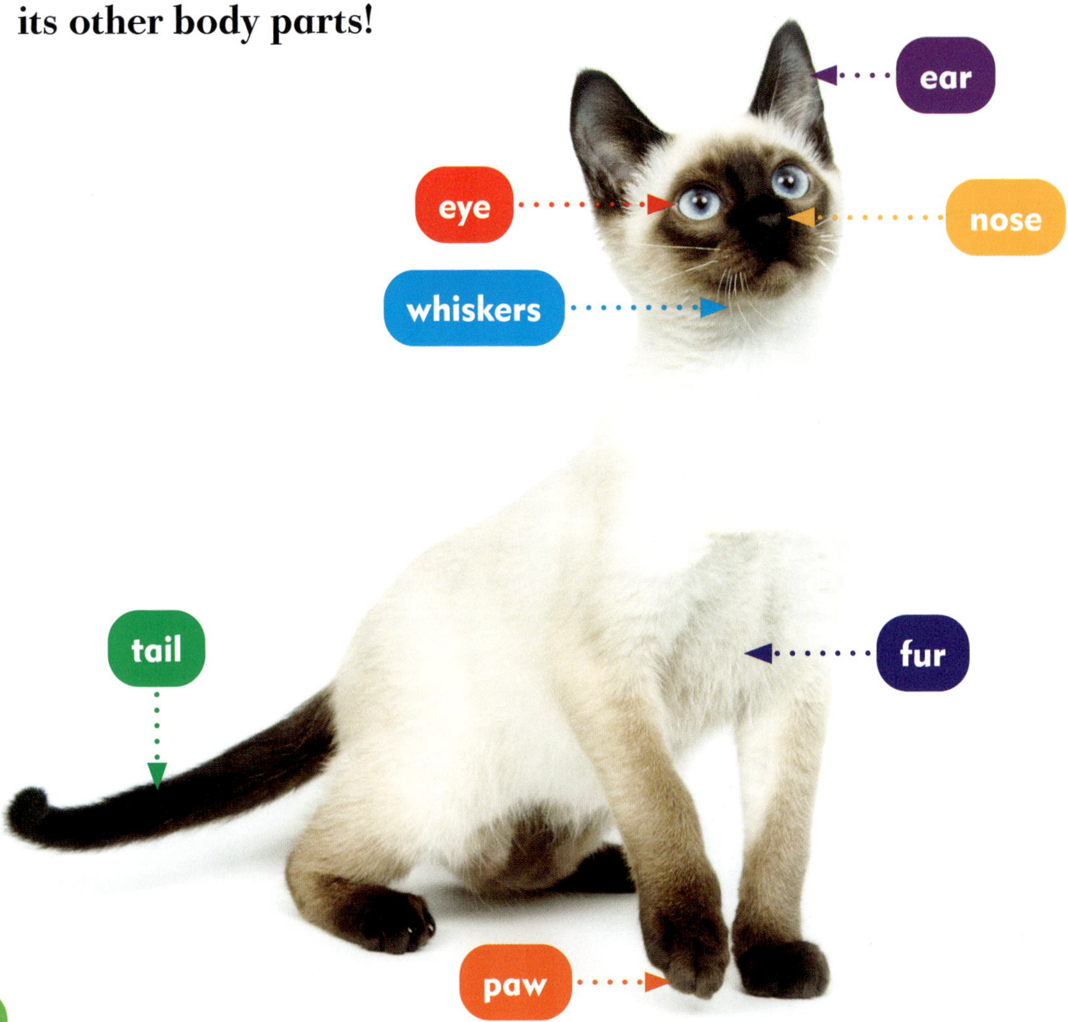

Picture Glossary

active
Energetic and busy.

curious
Eager to know or learn about something.

perch
A raised place where a cat can sit.

point pattern
A color pattern in which fur on the face, tail, legs, and ears is darker.

pounce
To jump forward and grab something suddenly.

purrs
Makes a low, vibrating sound in the throat.

Index

To Learn More

Finding more information is as easy as 1, 2, 3.

1. Go to www.factsurfer.com
2. Enter "Siamese" into the search box.
3. Click the "Surf" button to see a list of websites.